This
Treasure Cove Story
belongs to

THE TEAPOT'S TALE

A CENTUM BOOK 978-1-912396-12-2
Published in Great Britain by Centum Books Ltd.
This edition published 2018. 1 3 5 7 9 10 8 6 4 2

Centum Books Ltd, 20 Devon Square, Newton Abbot,
Devon, TQ12 2HR, UK.

www.centumbooksltd.co.uk | books@centumbooksltd.co.uk
CENTUM BOOKS Limited Reg.No. 07641486.

A CIP catalogue record for this book is available
from the British Library.

Printed in China.

A Treasure Cove Story

DISNEY
PRINCESS

Beauty and the Beast
The Teapot's Tale

Adapted by Justine Korman
Illustrated by Peter Emslie and Darren Hunt

Hello! My name is Mrs Potts. I wasn't always a teapot – heavens no! All of us in this castle were put under a strange spell some years ago by a powerful enchantress. She turned the young prince into a terrible beast because he was selfish and cruel.

There was only one way the prince could break the spell.
The enchantress gave him a magic rose that would bloom
until his twenty-first birthday. The prince would remain
a beast unless he could learn to love and be loved before
the last petal fell from the rose.

Lonely years passed while the Beast hid from the world. He refused to leave the castle. He didn't even want any tea. I tried to stay cheerful, but there's nothing sadder than an empty teapot – except an empty teacup like my poor son, Chip.

Then one stormy day an old man who was lost in the woods found his way to the castle. Lumière the candlestick and Cogsworth the clock let him in and brought him to the fireplace. He was cold and wet and I was so happy to offer him a hot cup of tea. 'It'll warm you up in no time,' I said.

But the master was boiling mad! He hated anyone to see him in his beastly form. 'So! You came to stare at the Beast, did you?' the Beast raged.

'I just needed a place to stay,' the old man explained.

'I'll give you a place to stay!' the Beast roared and he locked the poor man away in the tower.

Under his rages, I knew the Beast had a kind heart. But I worried that he would never learn to control his temper. And if he didn't learn to love before long, I would stay a teapot forever.

Soon after the old man's arrival, Chip babbled,
'Mama, Mama, there's a girl in the castle!'
'Now, Chip,' I scolded, 'I'll not have you making
up such wild stories.'
But it was true! The girl's name was Belle and she
had come to rescue her father – the man in the tower.

Belle was frightened by the Beast, but she had offered
to stay in her father's place. Her father was worried, but
the Beast sent him home.

Belle did stay. She was such a pretty girl. We all
bubbled with excitement. If only she and the master
would fall in love and break the spell!

Chip and I went straight to Belle's room. It chilled me to the spout to see her so sad. We tried to cheer her up. 'Things will turn out right in the end,' I assured Belle. 'You'll see.'

How the master raged when Belle refused to come
down to dinner with him! I told him, 'Try to be patient,
sir. After all, the girl has lost her freedom and her father
in one day.'

But the Beast roared, 'If she won't eat with me, then
she won't eat at all!'

Despite the master's orders, Belle dined on the best the castle had to offer. I'd rather have broken my own handle then let such a lovely child go hungry. The rest of the staff felt the same way. When Belle came downstairs later than night, we served her the most wonderful meal she had ever eaten.

Lumière and the others put on quite a show! Just having a guest made us overflow with joy! I warmed myself up and poured Chip full. We did our best to make Belle feel at home.

But one day Belle ran way. The Beast had flown into
a rage when he found Belle in his private room. She
was terrified.

Belle didn't get far before she was surrounded by
wild wolves. The master rescued her, though the wolves
savagely clawed and bit him.

Back at the castle, we watched as Belle tended the master's wounds. She was very gentle. When she thanked him for saving her life, my eyes steamed with tears. A tingle of hope tickled my spout.

I told Cogsworth, 'There may be something here that wasn't there before.'

Indeed there was! I nearly flipped my lid. For the first time in his life, the master wanted to do something special for someone else. Belle loved to read, so the master told her she could have any of the books in his wonderful library.

Chip was too young to understand, but I knew the feelings between Belle and the master had changed. I felt all warm inside – even though I wasn't anywhere near the stove.

Oh, but the course of true love never does run smoothly. Belle discovered that her father was ill. She begged the Beast to let her go home and the master allowed her to leave the castle.

While Belle was taking care of her sick father, trouble was brewing in the village.

A wicked hunter convinced the villagers that the Beast would soon attack their homes. So they decided to attack the Beast first. We heard the hunter shout, 'Kill the Beast!' The next thing we knew, the townspeople were storming the castle.

The servants defended the castle. But the master
wouldn't lift a paw to help us. He was brokenhearted
about Belle having gone away.

While we servants fought in our own special way, the
evil hunter attacked the master. The Beast couldn't find
the strength to fight back until he heard Belle's voice.
She had returned!

Before he fell from the castle wall, the hunter had stabbed the Beast in the back. We all feared he would die. Belle leaned over the master and cried, 'Don't leave me. I love you!'

But it was too late. Or was it?

Suddenly magic sparks filled the air. The Beast seemed to float off the ground. Rays of light shot from his paw as they changed into hands and feet. Right in front of my eyes, the master became a handsome prince!

And I... I turned back into my old self again and so did dear little Chip and everyone else in the castle. The curse over us was broken by the magic of true love.

Soon after that, Chip asked me a question. 'Mama, are Belle and the prince going to live happily ever after?'

I nodded and gave him a big hug. We're living happily ever after too, but since those days, I've never taken a teapot for granted!

Treasure Cove Stories

Book list may be subject to change.

An ongoing series to collect and enjoy!